Noticed by My Bully's Dad: An Age Gap Romance

Isla Chiu

Published by Isla Chiu, 2024.

This is a work of fiction. Similarities to real people, places, or events are entirely coincidental.

NOTICED BY MY BULLY'S DAD: AN AGE GAP ROMANCE

First edition. July 3, 2024.

ISBN: 979-8227552556

Written by Isla Chiu.

Also by Isla Chiu

Alpha Male U
Dare
Safe
Professor
Casual

Indecent Proposals
Office Hours: A Student and Professor Story
Loving the Chase
Taken by the Casino Owner

OTT Enterprises
Dear Mr. CEO, I Want You
Dear Mr. CFO, I Hate You
Dear Mr. Counsel, I Need You
Dear Mr. Chairman, I Want to Have Your Baby

Standalone
His Sweet Little Addiction
Just Because of You
A Night with Paradise Four
Taking the Bride
You Equals Mine
Claiming His Runaway Bride
Catching His Thief: A Thanksgiving Insta-Love Story
Kidnapping the Bride
Ringing in the Lunar New Year
The Only One that I Want
The Obsessed Husband
Caught by the Men of the House
Call Me Oppa
Breaking His Rules
Taking Our Bride
Claiming Our Runaway Bride
Sparks Fly: A New Adult Friends to Lovers Romance
Her Cookies: A Student and Teacher Insta-love Story
Quick & Dirty: 3 Stories
Hello, Alpha Male: A Romance 5 Book Bundle
Tempting Him: A Dad's Best Friend Story
His Pretty Prisoner
He Knows What He Wants: A Romance 5 Book Bundle
Her Elegant Prison
Blackmailed by the Jerk
Alpha Male Blast from the Past
Caught in the Act
Compromising the Earl's Daughter

Obsessed with Her: A Romance Collection
Wanting His Student
Claimed on Halloween: A Vampire Romance
His Enchanting Princess
His Lovely Prisoner
My Best Friend Forever
A Werewolf Jock for Thanksgiving
Enchanted by You: A Romance Collection
To Have Her: An Alpha Male Romance Collection
You're Mine, Wife
Her Beautiful Captor: A Captive Romance Collection
His Exquisite Prisoner
My First Theft Went a Little Like This
A Werewolf Jock for the New Year
Taking Back My Bride
So Much More
My Immortal Valentine
Short and Not So Sweet: A Short Story Collection
Caught by Mr. Smith
Bad Habits: A MMF Romance
Claiming Lady Wynn
Compromised: A Romance Collection
Over the Moon(cake) for You
The Sweetest Revenge: An Age Gap Romance
Noticed by My Dad's Best Friend: An Age Gap Romance
Bought by My Best Friend's Dad: An Age Gap Romance
Mile High with My Dad's Best Friend: An Age Gap Romance
Dad's Former Best Friend Just Got Out of Prison: An Age Gap Romance
Bought by My Dad's Boss: An Age Gap Romance
Found by My Bully's Dad: An Age Gap Romance

Wanted by My Best Friend's Dad: An Age Gap Romance
Caught by the King: An Age Gap Romance
Saved by My Professor: An Age Gap Romance
Claimed by a Billionaire on Christmas Eve: An Age Gap Romance
Bought by My Bully's Dad: An Age Gap Romance
Older Than Me: An Age Gap Romance Collection
Wanted by My Ex-Boyfriend's Dad: An Age Gap Romance
Caught by My Dad's Boss: An Age Gap Romance
A Billionaire for Lunar New Year: An Age Gap Romance
To Be His: An Age Gap Romance Collection
Bought by the Billionaire: An Age Gap Romance
Caught by My Boyfriend's Dad: An Age Gap Romance
Discovered by My Best Friend's Dad: An Age Gap Romance
Caught with the King: An Age Gap Romance
Surprised by the Billionaire: An Age Gap Romance
Wedded to the Mobster: An Age Gap Romance
Noticed by My Boyfriend's Coach: An Age Gap Romance
Picked Up by the Mobster: An Age Gap Romance
Kidnapped by the Billionaire: An Age Gap Romance
Caught by My Professor: An Age Gap Romance
Working for My Dad's Best Friend: An Age Gap Romance
Waiting on My Dad's Former Friend: An Age Gap Romance
Trapped in the Storm With My Boyfriend's Dad: An Age Gap Romance
She's Mine: An Age Gap Romance Collection
Claimed by the Mountain Man: An Age Gap Romance
An Offer from My Dad's Creditor: An Age Gap Romance
Knocked Up by the Tycoon: An Age Gap Romance
Caught by the College President: An Age Gap Romance
Wanted by My Fake Boyfriend's Dad: An Age Gap Romance

An Offer from the CEO: An Age Gap Romance
Claimed by the Hotel Owner: An Age Gap Romance
Found by the Cowboy: An Age Gap Romance
Claimed by the Lawyer: An Age Gap Romance
Security Risk: An Age Gap Romance
Prom Night with My Boyfriend's Dad: An Age Gap Romance
Trapping the Billionaire: An Age Gap Romance
My Best Friend's Stepbrother: An Age Gap Romance
My Billionaire Ex-Boyfriend
The Mobster's Property: An Age Gap Romance
Pursued by the Club Owner: An Age Gap Romance
He's Obsessed: An Age Gap Romance Collection
Taken by the Senator: An Age Gap Romance
Alpha Male Alert: An Age Gap Romance Collection
Wanting the Intern: An Age Gap Instalove Romance
Noticed by My Bully's Dad: An Age Gap Romance

Table of Contents

To my bully's dad ;) Just kidding...maybe.

Author's Note

ALL CHARACTERS DEPICTED in this story are at least 18 years of age.

Noticed by My Bully's Dad

"YOU GOTTA BE KIDDING me," I say when I look at my bike–or what's left of it. The tires have been slashed to black ribbons, and the frame is in pieces. *POOR BITCH*, one of the aluminum pieces says in red paint.

Jacob fucking O'Connor–my ex and the guy who must have destroyed my bike. Or more precisely, the guy who paid someone to wreck my bike because the rich asshole doesn't like getting his own hands dirty.

My reputation, my textbooks, and now my bike–what else is the asshole going to take from me?

My boss Randy comes out of the restaurant. He widens his eyes at the pile of aluminum and rubber on the ground. "Is that your bike?"

I sigh. "Yeah."

He rubs the back of his head, avoiding eye contact. "Well, I would drive you home, but I got so much stuff in the car..."

Well, you could always move your stuff. But I don't say the words out loud because knowing my boss, he would accuse me of being "sassy" and threaten to cut my hours. And though I hate being a waitress at the Sideways Skirt, I need to hold on to every hour I can get. So I say, "I'll just walk home. Thanks anyway." *Thanks for absolutely nothing.*

"Shouldn't you call the cops?"

I shake my head. "It's not worth it. I was planning to get a new bike anyway." The second sentence is a lie because my "poor bitch" ass was banking on my bike getting me through all 4 years of college. However, the first sentence is all too true. Since O'Connor's family is filthy rich, he could strangle me and throw my corpse in front of the dean's office and maybe get a slap—nay, a light tap—on the wrist.

Randy nods. "All right. See you at work tomorrow?"

Unfortunately, yes. "See you tomorrow."

When I watch Randy drive away, I can't help noting how the back of his car seems to have plenty of space.

I look into the dark night, dread filling me at the walk ahead. My dorm is 3 miles away from the Sideways Skirt, a distance that isn't so bad on a bike. But 3 miles on your feet after you've spent 8 hours running around a restaurant filled with disrespectful male customers who think they're entitled to more than a friendly smile? Absolute hell. If only this town had a halfway decent public transportation system instead of a single bus that runs from noon to maybe 5 PM.

I let out a deep breath, gripping the pepper spray in my pocket.

Then I start walking. And continue walking. 5 blocks later, I am hexing Jacob O'Connor and all of his family.

"Hey, Lucy Liu!"

Though I stiffen, I keep on walking. At least once a month, some jerk calls me Lucy Liu. Don't these guys know any other Asian actresses?

"Hey, Lucy, why are you giving me the cold shoulder?"

Though my tired feet and legs are screaming, I quicken my pace.

Unfortunately, the guy is faster and soon seizes my wrist.

"Hey, Lucy, you really shouldn't ignore me," the guy says, his breath reeking of booze.

My heart beats hard against my chest as I look at his bloodshot eyes. *Don't panic. Remember, you have pepper spray in your pocket.* However, my dumb ass drops the pepper spray when I take it out of my pocket.

The guy's face darkens. "You were going to pepper spray me just for talking to you?"

And for touching me without my consent. "Look, I just want to–"

"Oh, hello, there you are."

My eyes pop out of their sockets when a second man wraps his arms around me. What the hell? Is today Harass Mina Zhou Day?

"Sorry I was late to meet you, dear," the silver-haired man says to me. He doesn't stink of alcohol, though I don't know if a sober man in control of all of his instincts is necessarily any safer. To the drunk guy, he asks, "Could you let go of my girlfriend?"

Drunk Guy snorts. "Girlfriend? She's more like your daughter, and you're like her fucking dad. You know, if you weren't white and she wasn't Asian."

Sober Guy sighs. "Well, I tried asking nicely." Then he tears Drunk Guy's hand off my wrist, and I hear a very audible crack when he squeezes Drunk Guy's fingers.

"Ow, ow, ow!" Drunk Guy squeals. "Okay, okay, okay, I'll leave your girlfriend alone! Just let me go!"

"Say please," Sober Guy says, squeezing Drunk Guy's hand again and producing another crack.

"Okay, okay, please, please, please!"

As soon as Sober Guy lets go, Drunk Guy runs away, though due to his intoxication, he stumbles twice.

Still holding me, Sober Guy looks down at me. "Are you okay?"

"Yeah, um, thanks," I say even as I think, *Are you going to pick up from where Drunk Guy left off?* I swallow, too aware of the stranger's strength—he crushed Drunk Guy's wrist like it was a goddamn tomato—and of how he's a foot (at least) taller than me.

He frowns. "A woman of your stature shouldn't be walking alone at night."

On the rare occasion when my posture is good, I'm maybe two inches over 5 feet. "I have pepper spray."

"Which is currently on the ground."

I flush as he picks it up and hands it to me. "Thanks."

"Let me drive you home."

One piece of advice my mama's drilled into me since I learned how to speak: *Don't get into a car with a strange man, even if he offers you money, ESPECIALLY if he offers you money.* "Thanks, but I don't live far from here," I say, even as my feet scream, *Bitch, you still have to walk at least 2 and a half miles.*

He narrows his eyes. "Define 'not far.'"

I swallow. "Um, like two-ish miles."

He grits his teeth. "You're not walking 2 miles by yourself." He seizes my hand and pulls me toward a gray Prius, his tight grip letting me know that he is much, *much* stronger than me. I take my pepper spray out of my pocket, and motherfucker, it falls out of my hand *again*.

He stops. After a moment of excruciatingly awkward silence, he asks, "Are you going to pick that up?"

I blink. I say oh-so eloquently, "Um..."

"If it makes you feel safer, you can keep your pepper spray aimed at me while I drive you home."

So I can spray mace into your eyes, causing you to lose control of the wheel and us to die in a fiery car crash? I look into his eyes. He doesn't give me bad vibes like Drunk Guy did. Of course, it doesn't hurt that he's good-looking with his chiseled jawline and gorgeous green eyes, but I swear, I'm not letting that affect my judgment (much).

I bend down to grab my pepper spray, but it turns out to be an embarrassingly long process because I keep dropping the damn thing. God, have I developed a medical condition that causes permanently buttery fingers?

He mutters, "For fucking Christ's sake," before picking up the pepper spray and wrapping my fingers tightly around the mace. "Don't drop it," he says to me like I'm a child who's been entrusted with the wedding rings.

My heartbeat races as he opens the passenger door of his car for me. Before I can change my mind and run away from him, he puts a hand on the small of my back and pushes, forcing me inside the Prius.

"I'm not going to hurt you," he says in a gruff voice.

His words fail to relax me by even one iota.

"Where am I taking you?" he asks, starting the car.

"You can drop me off at the Genevieve Boehm Library." It's only a few blocks away from my dorm.

"You'll be safe walking home from there?" he asks.

When I nod, he begins driving.

The walk back to campus would have taken an hour–and that's an optimistic estimate given how tired my short legs are after my long work shift–but the car ride takes less than 6 minutes.

"Thanks for the ride, Mister..." And I realize I have no idea what this guy's name is.

"You can call me Jake."

Something in me tightens at hearing the shortened version of Jacob. I know it's ridiculous, but my ex has utterly ruined that name for me. "Thanks, Jake." At least he doesn't go by Jacob like my ex.

"What's your name?"

"Mina."

"Mina," Jake says, his deep voice stretching out each syllable. "Are you sure your place isn't far from here?"

"It's a short walk." I don't think Jake is a creep, but I still don't think I should let a stranger know where I live.

"Have a good night, Mina."

"Have a good night, Jake."

After I get out of the car, I wave goodbye at him from the sidewalk. For a few moments, he just stares at me, keeping the car still.

I let my hand fall back to my side. Just as I start wondering if he is a creep and might try to follow me back to my dorm, he drives away.

Huh, he didn't ask for my number. I want to smack myself. For God's sake, did I even want him to ask for my number?

An annoying little voice in the back of my head answers, *Yes*.

"Whatever," I mutter. I doubt he found me attractive after he saw me struggle so much with picking up the pepper spray. Besides, he's way older than me, at least old enough to be my dad.

For all I know, he's a married man with a dozen kids, and despite whatever rumors my ex might start, I'm no homewrecker.

Speaking of Jacob O'Connor, guess who's waiting for me outside my dorm.

The smirk on my ex's face is begging for a hard slap. "How was the walk home?"

I try to walk past him and act like he doesn't exist, but the bastard grabs the sleeve of my jacket.

He asks again, "How was the walk home?"

I exhale, turning to look at him. Why did I ever date this asshole? I stare at his dark brown hair that's messy-but-in-a-sexy-way and the five o'clock shadow that's scruffy-but-in-a-sexy-way due to his flawless bone structure.

Oh right, because I'm a total sucker for a good-looking face. Still, even with that face, I could only date him for 2 months. We just had nothing in common. All he seemed to care about was lacrosse, something I only pretended to like for his sake. And when I tried to talk to him about something, anything else, 99% of the time, all he said to me was, "Oh, cool, babe." Seriously, that was it.

So when I broke up with him, I thought he wouldn't care since he didn't seem to like me that much anyway. But oh, he fucking cared. I didn't break his heart, but I did something worse–I hurt his ego. How could little poor me–who doesn't even have a trust fund and has to wait tables to pay for my textbooks–dump Jacob O'Connor, Boehm University's star lacrosse player and the son of one of the school's most generous donors?

As payback for bruising his ego, not only did he spread deepfakes and rumors calling me the Whore of Boehm, but he's also destroyed a bunch of my personal property including but not limited to textbooks, shoes, and most recently, my bike.

"The walk home was delightful," I say. "Really made me appreciate the late autumn breeze. May you please let go of me now?"

His grip on my sleeve tightens. "I can buy you a new bike."

I glare at him. "Why the hell would you do that? Is your conscience hurting after destroying my old bike? I didn't know you even had one."

"I can buy you a new bike...if you get back together with me."

For a second, I just stare at Jacob in silence, my jaw slack with shock. Then I burst into laughter. Wheezing, I ask, "You...you seriously think...I would...get back...together...with you...for a new bike?" My laughter dies down and is replaced by anger. "Do you think I'm that cheap? I wouldn't get back together with you for your fucking trust fund." And my ex has an eight-figure trust fund.

He hisses, "Fuck you."

"You wish," I hiss. "Why do you even want to get back together? You don't actually like me." I cock my head. "Do you just want me to get back together with you, so you can end up dumping me like I dumped you?"

His silence is affirmation.

"God, you're so predictable," I say. "Just leave me alone, Jacob." I know he won't though, and there's a 90% chance he'll destroy another thing of mine tomorrow.

Finally, I manage to yank my sleeve from his grasp and rush into my dorm, ignoring him calling after me.

In my room, I collapse onto the bed, groaning with exhaustion. It's been a long-ass day, and it's going to be a long-ass day tomorrow. I have another 8-hour shift at the restaurant, but before that, I have to get lunch with one of the university's donors. I'm a Boehm First-Generation Scholar, which is a fancy way of saying my family is too poor to pay Boehm University's absurdly expensive tuition. As a Boehm First-Generation Scholar, I get a generous need-based scholarship from the college. In order to continue receiving my scholarship, I have to maintain at least a 3.0 GPA and go on a fortnightly lunch date with one of the school's major donors. During these lunches, it's expected for me to express my immense gratitude to the donors for funding the First-Generation Scholar program–i.e., to kiss some wealthy ass.

These lunches are typically some level of excruciating–I had to listen to one donor talk about the intricacies of trade laws for *3 hours*–but at least I get some free meals.

Before I go to sleep, I should work on my problem set for Calculus. After all, that 3.0 GPA isn't going to maintain itself. However, I've only changed into my pajamas when my eyes start fighting to stay open, and it's not long before they lose that fight.

* * ❧ * *

I FEEL LIKE A ZOMBIE when I wake up at 11 AM. God, I hope this donor's chosen restaurant serves espresso. I'm going to need it, especially if this donor likes to drone on about something boring like trade law.

After I put on an outfit that doesn't consist of sweats, I head to the restaurant, which is a French place called Luxe Bistro. Though it's only 2 blocks away from my dorm, I've never stepped inside because the name of the restaurant is reflected in the menu prices (the average *sandwich* costs 30 bucks).

"Are you Miss Zhou?" the hostess asks.

I blink. "Yes, I'm Mina Zhou."

"Please follow me, Miss Zhou. Mr. O'Connor has requested a private room for the two of you."

I freeze. Mr. O'Connor—as in Jacob's dad? As in the father of the asshole who's been doing his damnedest to make my life hell on Earth?

The hostess raises her eyebrows. "Excuse me, Miss Zhou, are you all right?"

I shake my head. "Oh, sorry, yes, I'm all right."

"Then please follow me."

I drag my feet across the restaurant like I'm a French noble walking to the guillotine. Maybe it's another donor with the last name O'Connor. After all, it's not like O'Connor is an uncommon last name.

When I enter the private room, I see the stranger who gave me a ride last night sitting at the table.

Fuck.

"May I start you off with some drinks?" the hostess asks, oblivious to the panic rising inside me.

"I'd have a Bloody Mary," Jake-not-Jacob says. Shit, now that I'm looking at him, I realize that he has green eyes like Jacob-not-Jake.

"What do you want to drink, Mina?" Jake-not-Jacob asks when I haven't answered the hostess.

"Oh, um, do you have espresso?" I ask.

"Yes," she says, sounding vaguely insulted by my question.

"Could I have one shot of espresso? Actually, make that two."

"Two shots of espresso, got it." She glances at the table. "Um, do you want to sit down?"

No. But since I have to eat lunch with Mr. O'Connor to continue getting financial aid, I give her a sheepish smile and sit my poor ass down.

"So you made it home last night from the library?" Jake–aka the father of my ex and bully–asks.

"Yes, thanks again for giving me a ride, Mr. O'Connor." So Jacob is named after his dad and got his pretty green eyes. Did he also inherit his bad temper?

"Please call me Jake."

I muster up a smile. "Okay, Jake." I can't believe I found–still find–Jacob's dad attractive. Why didn't my gut go, *Bad vibes, girl, I think this guy might be the vengeful demon's sperm donor?*

"How do you like my alma mater so far?"

Oh, it's freaking fantastic except for the guy who's intent on destroying my reputation, my property, and my life. "I really enjoy my classes and professors. Especially Professor Tisdale, who teaches my creative writing class. She's brilliant." I want to go home and curl up in a ball.

"Glad to hear it. Making plenty of friends?"

Ha. "A few good ones," I lie. Hardly anyone is eager to be besties with the Whore of Boehm. A lot of my classmates preach sex positivity on their social media accounts, but do they practice what they preach? Nope. More than a few of these supposedly sex-positive classmates have whispered, "Slut," when they pass me on campus.

I twist my hands, wanting to ask him, *Do you know that your son is, like, the fucking worst and what he's done to me?* Instead, I ask, "Did you know who I was when you met me last night?"

"I did. Perhaps I should've told you who I was yesterday. My apologies."

"It's all right." *But based on your son's personality, you should maybe apologize for your parenting skills.* Suppressing a sigh, I say, "I want to express my immense gratitude. It's because of donors like you that students like me—"

He cuts me off with a wave. "I just write the school big checks. You don't need to thank me."

I blink. With other donors, I got the feeling that I could have thanked them on my knees for several hours, and that wouldn't have been enough. "Still, thank you. I really—"

"Please, consider your immense gratitude expressed."

When the server comes to take our orders, Jake says, "I would like the rack of lamb."

"And I would like, um, the bistro salad with chicken." At $22, it's the cheapest thing on the menu besides the bistro salad sans chicken, which costs $18. On my first scholarship-mandated lunch with a donor, I made the mistake of ordering the filet mignon, the most expensive thing on the menu. I thought it would be okay since the donor got filet mignon as well plus 2 lobster tails, but I caught her pursing her lips in displeasure when I told the waiter my order. I guess she was okay with spending money on my overpriced tuition and the idea of treating me to lunch. But treating me to *filet mignon*? Well, I'm just taking advantage of her generosity at that point.

Since then, I've learned that rich people can be stingy with the strangest things and kept my lunch orders modest.

Jake frowns. *Shit, should I have gotten the bistro salad sans chicken?* Then he asks, "Really? All you want is a salad?"

I flush. "The bistro salad sounded good." Really, it sounded like an average salad at a not-so average price.

He rolls his eyes. "I'm treating you to lunch. Order what you want."

I say hesitantly, "The duck a l'orange sounds good." When I see the eye-widening price tag, I add hastily, "Or maybe the steak frites–"

He tells the server, "Forget the salad. She'll have both the duck a l'orange and steak frites. Medium rare." He looks at me. "You like your steak medium rare?"

Picking up my jaw from the floor, I nod.

"Thank you, Jake," I say once it's just the two of us in the private room again.

"When you're with me, you can get whatever you want." He says the words like it's inevitable that we'll spend time together beyond this scholarship-mandated lunch. Why am I feeling something akin to excitement at the thought? I shouldn't want to spend more time with my bully ex's dad.

And I certainly shouldn't be looking at his dad's lips and wondering how they would feel on my mouth, among other body parts...

"How do you like your espresso?" he asks, his deep voice cutting through my horny imagination.

I hope in vain that my face isn't as red as an apple. "It's good. How's your Bloody Mary?"

"Delicious. Want to try some?"

"Oh, thank you, but I'm 19."

"Ah." He keeps his gaze on me as he takes another sip of his drink, and for some reason, I want to shiver.

Our food arrives. I take a bite of the duck a l'orange, and my taste-buds damn near explode.

Jake smiles. "I bet that's a lot better than the bistro salad."

I say with complete sincerity, "It's one of the best things I've ever tasted."

The steak is also marvelous and melts in my mouth like butter. God, I'm going to loathe dinner at the Sideways Skirt tonight. The food there is mediocre in general, but my boss insists on feeding his employees only dry burgers and soggy fries.

Halfway through the duck a l'orange and steak frites, I look at the time. My shift starts in an hour. That should be enough time...

Then I remember that I have to walk to the Sideways Skirt because Jake's son slaughtered my bike. I have to start hauling ass *now*.

"Sorry, I have to get going soon," I say. "I need to go to work."

"I can drive you."

My eyes light up. If he drives me, I can leave later and not have to let my lunch go to waste. Then I remind myself that I work at the Sideways Skirt. If you've never been, imagine Hooters with worse chicken wings and cheaper outfits. My work uniform consists of a crop top that covers my nipples (and little else) and a miniskirt that's always on the verge of exposing my underwear. Jake didn't see my uniform last night because I kept it hidden under my long jacket.

I say in a rush, "Oh, I don't want you to inconvenience yourself."

"Let me drive you to work *and* pick you up from work. It won't be an inconvenience." His voice becomes low. "But the thought of you walking alone at night inconveniences me very, very much."

I glance at the time and swallow. If I don't get going *now*, I'm definitely going to be late to work. Grabbing my purse, I say, "You really don't have..."

But I don't finish my sentence because my dumb ass drops my bag as I shoot up from the table, and what spills out of my purse and onto the floor robs me of the ability of speech.

For a pregnant pause, Jake gazes at the crop top and miniskirt. Maybe he doesn't recognize my uniform? However, my hopes are dashed when he says in a flat tone, "You work at the Sideways Skirt."

"Um, yeah. But it's not like it was my first choice! God, not at all! I tried to get a work-study job on campus, but all of my applications were rejected. I also called a few coffee shops, but no one was hiring. So I kind of had no choice–"

I gasp when Jake grabs my waist and pulls me down to his lap. He snarls, "You're not working there anymore."

"But–"

"Stay and finish your meal, or I'm going to tell the school that you didn't show up for lunch."

I gape at him. "But...but I have to go to work."

"Why do you need a part-time job? Isn't your scholarship supposed to cover your tuition and room and board?"

I scowl. "It doesn't cover textbooks." And it certainly doesn't cover the second set of textbooks I need to buy after the first set was destroyed by some of his son's minions. I continue, "And what if I want to get myself the occasional treat? So what if I'm poor? That doesn't mean I should deny myself Ferrero Rocher! We poors deserve nice chocolate too!"

Instead of saying something along the lines of *Sorry for trying to make you choose between your job and your scholarship; I am a jerk who needs to check his fucking privilege,* he replies, "You consider Ferrero Rocher to be nice chocolate?"

Apparently, both the father and son are elitist dickheads. "It's very nice chocolate," I hiss.

"I'll buy you your textbooks and all the Ferrero Rocher your heart desires."

I blink. "Huh?"

"So you no longer need to work at the Sideways Skirt." He gestures toward my half-eaten lunch. "Now finish your duck a l'Orange and steak, and feel free to savor each bite. No, you *have* to savor each bite."

I bristle at his bossy tone, but I don't want to let the delicious food go to waste, so I begrudgingly obey him. Maybe if I grovel to my boss Randy hard enough and offer to wash the dishes/ clean the toilets/take out the trash/et cetera, he won't fire me for being late. I try to get up, but Jake keeps an arm secured around my waist while sliding my plate over. Does he expect me to finish my lunch while sitting on his lap?

He puts my fork in my hand. I guess he does.

I shoot Mr. O'Connor a dirty look before taking a bite of duck. Though I'm irritated, I don't entirely hate sitting on his lap. It might just be the endorphins from the tasty food talking, but Jake is warm and smells good. I have no idea what notes his undoubtedly expensive cologne is composed of, but whatever they are, my nose takes pleasure in them.

Maybe a little too much pleasure.

Heat floods my face when the waiter walks in on us. To his credit, he doesn't betray any surprise except for a nearly imperceptible raise of his eyebrows. "How was your meal?"

"Wonderful," Jake says.

"Would you care for any dessert?"

Before I can say, *No, thank you,* Mr. O'Connor says, "We'll have the vanilla creme brulee." When he feels me squirm, the jerk adds, "And some raspberry macarons."

Once the server leaves, Jake says, "I told you, you no longer need to work at that restaurant." He wrinkles his nose. "If you can call a place like that a restaurant."

"But–"

He cuts me off, "You're not working at the Sideways Skirt anymore."

I let out an exasperated breath. "You can't just–"

However, I don't finish my sentence because Mr. O'Connor cuts me off again–this time, by putting his mouth over mine.

I stiffen as he tastes my lips. Is my ex's father *kissing* me right now? And if he is, why am I not punching him in the groin? Why am I closing my eyes and opening my lips? Why am I letting his tongue go past my lips and taste each inch of my mouth?

And why am I enjoying it so fucking much?

I hear the server clear his throat. "Here are the macarons and creme brulee," he says.

Without a hint of shame, Mr. O'Connor says, "Thank you. May you leave us right now?"

The waiter bows his head. "Of course, sir."

As soon as the server is gone, Jake tries kissing me again, but I clap my hand over his mouth. "What are you doing?"

Against my palm, he answers, "Distracting you from thinking about your former job."

My hand twitches with the urge to slap him. Taking my hand off his mouth, I shove a macaron past my lips before he can kiss me again.

"How's the macaron?" he asks.

"Terrible," I lie. It's fucking heavenly.

He chuckles, taking a macaron for himself. "You can insult me, but don't insult the restaurant."

I glare at him. "Okay. This macaron is absolutely delicious, but you're an asshole."

"I'm an asshole for not wanting you to work at a restaurant that exploits young women? Got it."

If the macarons weren't so delightful, I would throw one at his head.

He brings a spoon to my lips. "Want to try the creme brulee?"

I want to tell him that he can shove the spoon up his elitist ass, but I also really want to try the creme brulee. A pauper like me doesn't exactly have many opportunities to have creme brulee. I open my lips, letting him put the dessert in my mouth. I have to suppress a moan like I'm on the verge of having an orgasm in public.

"Good?" he asks with a smirk.

Nearly breathless from the effort to stop myself from moaning, I murmur, "Yes."

When a bit of the rich custard dribbles down my chin, he lowers his head and licks the dessert off my face.

"Are you this inappropriate with all of the scholarship students you take to lunch?" I ask. I feel a maddening rush of jealousy at the idea of him licking creme brulee off someone else. My conscience scolds me, *You shouldn't feel jealous. You should feel pity toward this hypothetical student he might be preying on.*

"No." The smirk drops from his face. "Are donors inappropriate with you?"

"Only you. *Other* donors maintain appropriate boundaries."

"I'm going to tell the school you can only have these lunches with me from now on."

I gawk at him. "Why?"

He holds my hips possessively. "To ensure *other* donors keep maintaining appropriate boundaries."

First, I attracted the attention and experienced the wrath of the son. And now, I've attracted the attention of the father. May God have mercy on my soul if I ever experience the wrath of the father.

After we finish dessert, the waiter brings us the check. Without seeming to even glance at the check, Jake tosses a few hundred-dollar bills on the table. "Keep the change," he tells our server before standing up and carrying me out of the restaurant.

"Put me down," I say with flushed cheeks, all too aware of how people are sneaking looks at us.

He sets me on my feet, then seizes my hand.

I glare at his large hand, which practically swallows up my microscopic-in-comparison hand. "Do you have to hold my hand?"

"How else am I going to ensure that you don't run off to the Sideways Skirt?" he asks, walking and pulling me along with him.

"Where are we going?"

"To the bookstore."

"Wait, you're actually buying me textbooks?"

He looks at me like I just said the Earth was flat. "Of course I am." Once we're inside the bookstore, he asks, "What books do you need?"

"You shouldn't…" I trail off when I see Sabrina Lane looking at us while pretending she's not looking at us. She's a fellow sophomore and a proud member of Boehm University's Sex Positivity Club. Yet more than once, I've heard her fake a cough while whispering, "Skank," in my presence. Not very sex-positive of her if you ask me.

I catch the hint of a smirk on her face. She must think Mr. O'Connor is my sugar daddy or a married man I'm sleeping with or something along those scandalous lines.

Better for her to think that than to recognize him as my ex's daddy.

"I'm writing checks that indirectly pay for your tuition," he says. "Why shouldn't I directly pay for your textbooks?"

It's hard to argue with his logic, and I don't. Besides, at this point, I don't think I have much of a choice. I rattle off the names of the textbooks for Calculus II, Intro to Economics, and Biology. He picks up *new* copies of all of them, and the price tags make my eyes pop out of my head. The textbooks that Mr. O'Connor's son destroyed were used copies from stingy upperclassmen I had to haggle with, so they were about $50 a pop. If my ex had destroyed textbooks I'd bought new, I think I would've been compelled to murder him.

While we stand in the checkout line, Mr. O'Connor picks up several boxes of Ferrero Rocher chocolates.

I say, "You don't need to–"

He silences me with a glare. "Just say, 'Thank you, Jake.'"

I begrudgingly obey him.

After he purchases the books and chocolates, I think he'll let me go at last, but he tightens his grip on my hand outside the store.

"Um, thanks again for the textbooks," I say. "I should go to the library and get started on some homework."

He pulls me back to him when I try to take a step. "You can finish your homework at my place."

My eyes turn into slits. "I *can* finish my homework at your place, or I *will* finish it at your place?"

In answer, Jake directs me to the back of a car. This time, it's a much less eco-friendly Mercedes-Benz instead of a Prius. In the backseat, I scowl at him when he draws me onto his lap so that I'm straddling him.

"What is with you?" I ask. "Are you obsessed with girls half your age or something?"

Breezily, he says, "I'm obsessed with you," but his dark lustful gaze belies his light tone. It shouldn't excite and arouse me—for many reasons, including but not limited to, he's my dad's age (maybe even older), an asshole, and the dad of my vengeful ex—but try telling that to my sex, which is getting hot and wet as I become aware of his hardening cock under me.

He starts undoing the buttons on my coat, and I do nothing to stop him.

When my coat falls to the floor, he opens my blouse, exposing my black bra. He tugs at one of the cups. My heart races as his breath touches my bare breast.

"Hey, my eyes are up here," I whisper.

"Do you want me to stop?" he asks. Though his breath is warm on my skin, I shiver.

I *should* tell him to stop. I *should* not hook up with my ex's father in the back of a gas-guzzling Mercedes-Benz.

But *should* is not a synonym for want.

"I don't want you to stop," I say.

With a grunt, he rips off my bra, rendering the hooks useless in the process. When I open my mouth to scold him, he growls, "I'll buy you a dozen new bras," before claiming one of my nipples with his mouth. My annoyance vanishes as he tastes my breast. I writhe in his arms, getting hotter and wetter between my thighs. Then he thrusts a hand down my pants, drawing moans out of me when he rubs the thin cotton that stands between my pussy and his fingers.

"Your panties are fucking soaked," he says against my neck, rubbing the cotton harder and quicker.

"And your dick is fucking hard," I say, sliding up and down the bulge in his trousers.

He hisses, grabbing my hips and stilling me. "Don't make me come in my pants instead of your pretty little cunt," he says, tearing open my panties.

"I hope you're planning to buy me new underwear along with the new bras."

"I'll buy you a fucking whole new wardrobe." He lets out his cock, the tip of which is already sticky with a little cum.

I scream out his name when his erection enters me. He wraps his arms around me like a vise, pushing his cock deep inside my pussy. Just as I start riding his dick, he pulls out, eliciting a mortifying little whimper from me.

He smirks. "Want to come, Mina?" He teases me by sliding his cock into my sex before pulling out again.

I almost beg, *Yes please.* Instead I whisper into his ear, "Not as much as you want to come inside my pretty little cunt."

"You're damn right about that," he snarls, burying his prick inside my pussy. I groan, digging my nails into his shoulders as he spills his sticky arousal onto my walls. Our bodies shudder against each other when my sex squeezes his cock.

"Come for me, Mina," he says.

I obey him, crying out as I coat his manhood with my juices and he fills me up with his hot white seed.

"We're home," he says. With his dick still inside me, he carries me out of the car. In the time it takes for me to say, "What the hell are you doing? Let me get dressed first, you asshole," we've entered his house, which is a white-columned brick mansion.

"You were saying?" he says, discarding what's left of my clothing on the steps while he carries me up a long staircase.

I shoot daggers at him as he takes us into a large bedroom. "Never mind," I mutter when he sets my naked body down on a king size bed.

He caresses my stomach. "Let me know if your period is late."

"Um, okay, but why would my period be late?"

He stares at me like I just told him that toys come alive when we're not looking. "Because I came inside you."

I burst into laughter. "I'm on birth control," I say. "Were you planning to knock me up?" When a vaguely guilty silence emanates from him, I gasp in indignation. "You were! Do you have a breeding kink or something, you dirty old man?"

He grasps the small of my back. "I want to make you mine."

"So what, your plan was, like, to knock me up and have a shotgun wedding?"

He says without a single ounce of shame, "Yes."

Dear God, he's obsessed with me, though we met yesterday.

But I have to admit I don't hate being the object of his obsession like I hate being the object of his son's obsession. Jacob only became obsessed with me *after* I dumped him. When we were together, he didn't even want to call me his girlfriend because he thought that "labels are so restrictive." Yet his dad is ready to call me his future wife.

Jake moves to kiss me, but I shove his chest before our lips can make contact. "I have to do homework. My GPA isn't going to maintain itself." When he opens his mouth, I add, "Don't offer to pay for my tuition if my GPA drops."

He sighs. "I'll get your textbooks and bag from the car." He strokes my cheek. "Don't go anywhere."

Before I can reply, *Where the hell would I go without any clothes?* he saunters out of the room.

I look around my surroundings, then pale when I see the framed photo on Jake's desk. In the picture, he's proudly standing next to Jacob wearing a graduation cap and gown. Welp, if I had any doubt that Jacob was Jake's son, that doubt has evaporated into nothing.

When Jake comes back with my bag, books, and coat, I stand up and say, "I should go." I can't be in a relationship or whatever this is with my bully's dad. If I thought my ex was a vengeful asshole before, who knows what he will do if he finds out I fucked his dad?

The edges of Jake's mouth curve down. "I told you, you're not working at the Sideways Skirt anymore."

"I'm not going there," I say, rifling through my bag. "I do need to put on the uniform though..."

"Why the hell do you need to do that?"

I narrow my eyes at him. "Because a certain someone destroyed the rest of my clothes."

He snatches the crop top and miniskirt out of my hands, and in one effortless motion, tears them in half.

I gawk at him. "What the fuck?"

"You're not going to that restaurant ever again."

I roll my eyes. "Okay, whatever, but I need to go." I grab my coat, which is at least long enough to cover my private parts.

The jerk yanks it out of my hands before ripping it into two.

"Jesus fucking Christ!" I exclaim.

He tosses the pieces of my coat onto the floor. "Did you get that coat at the dollar store? Ripping it should not have been that easy."

I didn't get it from the dollar store, but I did get it off the clearance rack in a thrift store for $5. "You're such a fucking asshole." Just like his son.

He wraps his arms around me. "I may be, but you're not going anywhere." He lifts my chin up. "Now tell me what's wrong. You were looking pale when I walked in."

I snarl, "I realized how big of a jerk you are."

"Mina, I think you realized that well before you came into this house."

I take a deep breath. The truth has to drive him away. What kind of father wants his son's sloppy seconds? "I used to date Jacob."

He lifts his eyebrows. "Jacob?"

I point at the framed photo on his desk. "Jacob, your son, the guy in that picture. We dated for, like, two months."

Instead of throwing his arms off me in disgust, he asks, "So? Were you two serious?"

I blink. "Well, no."

"Then I don't see why there should be a problem. We're all mature adults."

I snort. "Do you know your son?"

Jake knits his brow. "What is that supposed to mean?"

I throw up my hands. "I ended things with Jacob. We just couldn't talk about anything. I thought it wouldn't be a big deal because he didn't even want to call me his girlfriend. But when I dumped him, I think his brain broke or something because he went absolutely berserk and decided to do anything he can to ruin my life."

"What do you mean, ruin your life?"

I laugh. "Oh, where should I start? How about circulating deepfakes of me doing all kinds of salacious things with all kinds of men? Or paying people to rip up my textbooks? That's why I had to get new ones, by the way. Or hiring someone to chop up my bike? I wasn't walking home last night because I wanted to feel the autumn breeze."

"Is all of that true?" he asks in a low voice.

"Do you think I'm lying?" I shake my head. Why would he believe me? I'm just a random girl who's telling him that his only child is a terrible person. "Whatever. Me being here with you—it's just not a good idea." I try to push him away, but he tightens his embrace.

"I told you, you're not going anywhere."

I punch his arms, but it's like hitting tree trunks. "Do you know what your son will do to me if he finds out about us?" I don't know either, but I sure as hell don't want to find out.

Jake says coolly, "He won't do anything aside from being perfectly cordial to you. If he does anything that causes you even the tiniest bit of distress again, I will donate his entire trust fund to a nonprofit organization of your choice." His jaw tightens. "I might do that anyway. The things he's already done are beyond heinous. Fucking Christ, deepfakes?"

I widen my eyes. "You believe me, just like that?"

"Why would you lie to me?"

"I don't know, maybe I'll ask you to donate your son's trust fund to a bogus charity that's one of my offshore bank accounts."

Faint amusement comes over his face. "You had a coat from the dollar store. You don't have an offshore bank account."

"Excuse me, it was a coat from the *thrift* store." I can't help being touched by his trust in me. "Still, I should go. I don't want to get between you and your son."

He picks me up like I weigh as much as a bag of feathers. "How many times do I need to tell you that you're not going anywhere?" He tucks me under the comforter on the bed. "Do your homework. I'll talk to Jacob."

The door hits the wall with a loud thud as someone bursts into the room.

Damn, we summoned him like a demon, I think as Jacob focuses his hateful stare on me.

"You!" he hisses. "When Sabrina told me that she saw you with my dad, I didn't want to believe it."

I curse Sabrina with a semester of bad grades.

Jacob continues, "I didn't think that even a slut like you could sleep with–"

Though I've developed immunity to Jacob calling me names, his father bellows, *"Don't call Mina that."*

For a moment, my ex is stunned. But his silence doesn't last for long. "Dad, what kind of bullshit has she told you? You can't trust anything she says."

Without glancing at his son, Mr. O'Connor says, "Mina, I'm going to talk with my son." He kisses me on the cheek, which causes my ex to seethe. "I'll be right back."

The father and son go into the room next door. Unable to resist the urge to eavesdrop, I place my ear against the wall. I can't hear anything Jake is saying, but I catch my ex's side of the conversation since Jacob is very much not using his inside voice.

"Dad, you can't believe anything that girl says!"

"Okay, I was a bit upset by the breakup, but I had nothing to do with those deepfakes!"

"So what if I did? Why the hell should you care? It's not like she's anything to you."

"YOU'RE CUTTING ME OFF? YOU CAN'T GIVE AWAY MY TRUST FUND!"

"Dad, please don't do this to me! I'll do anything!"

"I can't believe you're siding with her over your only son!"

"Fine, I'll do whatever that she-devil wants."

Father and Son come back into the room. My ex glares at the pillow next to me like it just took a dump on his sports car.

Mr. O'Connor says, "Jacob has agreed to whatever penance you see fit."

I stare at Jacob. "Whatever I want?"

Jacob says through gritted teeth, "Whatever you want."

"I want you to leave me alone," I say. "No destroying my property, no showing up at my dorm unexpectedly, no getting your buddies to spread nasty rumors about me. I want to go to college in peace."

"All right."

I tap the bed, thinking. After a moment, I say, holding back a grin, "I want you to buy me a new bike, and I want it to be a real nice one."

He pulls out his wallet. "Okay, whatever, I'll just order one now–"

I hold up a finger. "Don't order one yet. You can't use your daddy's credit card or trust fund to get me a new bike."

He blinks, utterly confused. "How am I supposed to buy it then?"

My lips twitch with the urge to smile. "With wages from a part-time job at a fast-food establishment of your choice."

He gapes at me. "What? I don't have time for a job. I'm too busy with lacrosse!"

I say dryly, "Yet you somehow find time to attend several parties every week."

My ex scowls at me. His dad, on the other hand, looks like he's about to explode with laughter. "Fine, whatever, I'll work at some shitty fast-food place."

"Please let me know where you end up working," I say. "I would *love* for you to wait on me. And save up for an expensive bike. I can wait since I'm sure your daddy won't mind giving me rides in the meantime."

Jacob clenches his fist. I'm sure he would be tempted to punch me if his dad weren't in the room. "Well, is that it, Mina?"

I smile. "That's it."

He raises his hand in the world's most passive-aggressive wave. "I'll get going now. I apparently need to get started on job applications. See you later, Dad."

Once Jacob leaves, Mr. O'Connor says, sounding amused, "'I'm sure your daddy won't mind giving me rides in the meantime'?"

"It's true, isn't it?"

He rips the comforter off me. "It's true."

I catch my breath when he lowers his head and kisses my knee. "I...I need to start my homework."

His lips touch my thighs. "Your homework can wait."

I shudder as he lays a kiss on my clit, which is still sticky with his cum. I whisper, "Yes, it can wait." He sucks my nub clean of his white seed. I cry out, arching my back and thrusting my pussy against his face. He drives his tongue deep into my sex, licking his cum off my walls before lapping up my juices like they're glasses of champagne at a brunch buffet.

His breath is hot on my pussy as he grips my hips possessively. "I don't think I can ever get enough of your sweet cunt."

"I don't think I can ever get enough of you," I whisper.

He chuckles. "Good, because I'm never going to leave you alone, Mina." Then he resumes tongue-fucking me. I grab the back of his skull, murmuring his name over and over again as he plunges his tongue deeper and deeper inside me.

Soundless screams of ecstasy climb out of my throat when I come into his thirsty mouth. He slurps up every drop of my wet heat like it's exquisite honey.

"Oh, can you please do that again?" I ask, half-joking, half-dead-serious.

He raises his head. "After you finish your homework."

I've never completed a Calculus problem set so fast.

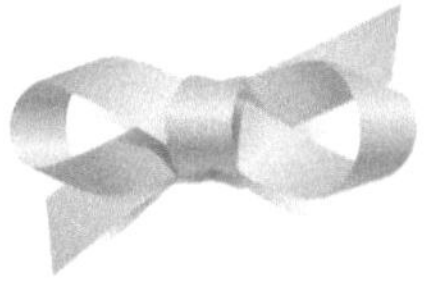

Epilogue

2 AND A HALF YEARS later

"Oh shit," I say when I see the two lines appear on the stick in my hand. In spite of me taking the pill at precisely 4:38 PM every day, I am pregnant.

Though the positive result makes me nervous as hell–I'm 22; I know next to nothing about raising a baby–not an ounce of unhappiness pumps through my blood. I want to have the baby, and I want to raise them with my boyfriend Jake O'Connor. Over the past few years, he's proposed to me a dozen times. Though I love him, I turned him down a dozen times because I wanted to graduate from college before becoming his wife.

However, since I'm set to graduate with a bachelor's degree in economics in less than a month and we now have a baby on the way, I think I'm poised to accept his inevitable 13th proposal.

An involuntary laugh leaves my lips. Christ, I'm carrying my ex Jacob's half-brother, and I might become Jacob's *stepmother* in the near future.

For a while, I was worried that my ex would try to drive a wedge between me and his dad, but he's managed to behave himself. We still dislike each other very much, but we alternate between being civil to each other and acting like the other doesn't exist. And he did end up following through on the penance I set for him. For the rest of college, I didn't hear one person calling me a slut or skank or ho. I even managed to make a few good friends.

And my ex did get me a new bike. He got me a lovely $1,000 bike with the paychecks he earned flipping burgers at Green & Clean. I went to Green & Clean once to see my ex in action, but as Green & Clean is a vegan fast-food joint that specializes in "guilt-free" (i.e., taste-free) quinoa burgers, I didn't feel the need to go a second time.

I go down the staircase. After the first semester of my sophomore year, I moved into Jake's mansion. Let me tell you, what an upgrade from the college dorms.

When I'm on the first floor, my stomach growls as I catch the scent of sizzling jade tofu, one of my favorite things to eat in the whole wide world. I walk to the dining room and see that Jake has laid out a feast on the table. In addition to sizzling jade tofu, there are spicy wontons, lobster with ginger scallion noodles, and a chiffon cake with whipped cream and fruit. "What's the special occasion?" I ask as he pours out two glasses of a bubbly beverage.

"You're pregnant."

My jaw drops. "How...?" I read the label on the bubbly beverage's bottle. Sparkling apple juice.

"I noticed your period was late."

"You keep track of my cycle? Creep."

"I'm simply an observant boyfriend." He takes my hand and slips a familiar ring onto my finger. It's the 6-carat diamond he's proposed to me with a dozen times. "Soon to be an observant husband."

I tease, "What makes you think I'm going to say yes this time?"

He frowns. "Mina..."

"I'm kidding." I hug him. "I would love to be your wife, Jake, and raise this child with you."

My words turn his frown upside down. "I love you."

"I love you too."

THE END

Sign up for my newsletter to get a free book!

GET *In the Dark: An Insta-Love Story* for free if you sign up for my newsletter here[1]. In addition, you'll hear about my new releases and get access to exclusive sales/freebies!

---

1. https://storyoriginapp.com/giveaways/5fbe502e-1570-11eb-a09f-67946e2bdeae

Connect with Me!

THANK YOU SO MUCH FOR reading! <3 If you enjoyed this story, please consider leaving a review.

If you want to connect with me, you can do so via the following platforms.

Goodreads: https://www.goodreads.com/author/show/17011380.Isla_Chiu

Email: islachiu@gmail.com

Don't miss out!

Visit the website below and you can sign up to receive emails whenever Isla Chiu publishes a new book. There's no charge and no obligation.

https://books2read.com/r/B-A-TNDF-PHUPD

BOOKS 2 READ

Connecting independent readers to independent writers.

Did you love *Noticed by My Bully's Dad: An Age Gap Romance*?
Then you should read *She's Mine: An Age Gap Romance Collection*[1] by Isla Chiu!

Warning: this collection contains 5 sexy age gap romance short stories featuring young women and their determined alpha males! Includes

Claimed by a Billionaire on Christmas Eve, Bought by My Bully's Dad, Wanted by My Ex-Boyfriend's Dad, Caught by My Dad's Boss, and *A Billionaire for Lunar New Year*!

Claimed by a Billionaire on Christmas Eve

---

1. https://books2read.com/u/3J6D1e

2. https://books2read.com/u/3J6D1e

I'm such a moron. I consider begging him for mercy, but frankly, I'm too tired to attempt to appeal to a rich guy's forgiving side. "So...are you going to hand me over to the cops?"

He strokes my cheek, making a shiver climb down my spine. To be honest, the shiver isn't entirely out of fear. He's handsome, a partially silver fox with silky waves of brown and gray hair, dark eyes that possess panty-melting heat, and a sexy five o'clock shadow on his strong jawline.

Jesus Christ, Krystal, this guy is old enough to be your dad, a voice in my head hisses. The reminder does nothing to lessen my attraction. Then the voice reminds me that this guy is going to have me arrested, and *that* reminder is like a cold shower.

He murmurs, "That depends on how agreeable you are."

Bought by My Bully's Dad

The auctioneer claps his hands, absolutely delighted. "Marvelous! Do I have $130,000? Going once, going twice—!"

"One million dollars."

I nearly faint when a man with streaks of gray in his chestnut hair stands up. He is gorgeous, the owner of brilliant green eyes, a bone structure that looks like it was sculpted by Donatello, and a muscular body that is complemented by his tailored black suit.

And he is Henry Lucas, the father of my bully.

Wanted by My Ex-Boyfriend's Dad

I swallow, my mouth turning dry. Stupidly, I think, *Wow, Mr. Radell is hot.* My ex-boyfriend's good looks didn't come out of nowhere. Like Geoff Radell III, Geoff Radell II has a mesmerizing green eye and an equally mesmerizing blue eye, messy and luscious auburn hair, and a five o'clock shadow on his impossibly defined jawline.

"Um, hi, I'm Lan Wu, your son's girlfriend," I say. To my horror, I begin babbling: "Well, ex-girlfriend. He cheated on me with a girl who thinks Helen Keller wasn't a real person. I only came here to get my laptop, not to do any revenge vandalism or anything."

The corner of his mouth quirks up. "Now I think you *did* come here to do some revenge vandalism."

Caught by My Dad's Boss

"What are you doing?"

I yelp, dropping the book. I cringe when the novel lands with a thud.

He clicks his tongue. "You shouldn't be so careless with that book. It's worth quite a bit of money."

My fear nearly strangles me as I turn around...

And see Stephen Cohen smirking at me. Although I've never formally met my dad's boss, I recognize him from seeing him in magazines.

Like an idiot, I squeak, "Hi."

Also by Isla Chiu

Alpha Male U
Dare
Safe
Professor
Casual

Indecent Proposals
Office Hours: A Student and Professor Story
Loving the Chase
Taken by the Casino Owner

OTT Enterprises
Dear Mr. CEO, I Want You
Dear Mr. CFO, I Hate You
Dear Mr. Counsel, I Need You
Dear Mr. Chairman, I Want to Have Your Baby

Standalone
His Sweet Little Addiction
Just Because of You
A Night with Paradise Four
Taking the Bride
You Equals Mine
Claiming His Runaway Bride
Catching His Thief: A Thanksgiving Insta-Love Story
Kidnapping the Bride
Ringing in the Lunar New Year
The Only One that I Want
The Obsessed Husband
Caught by the Men of the House
Call Me Oppa
Breaking His Rules
Taking Our Bride
Claiming Our Runaway Bride
Sparks Fly: A New Adult Friends to Lovers Romance
Her Cookies: A Student and Teacher Insta-love Story
Quick & Dirty: 3 Stories
Hello, Alpha Male: A Romance 5 Book Bundle
Tempting Him: A Dad's Best Friend Story
His Pretty Prisoner
He Knows What He Wants: A Romance 5 Book Bundle
Her Elegant Prison
Blackmailed by the Jerk
Alpha Male Blast from the Past
Caught in the Act
Compromising the Earl's Daughter

Obsessed with Her: A Romance Collection
Wanting His Student
Claimed on Halloween: A Vampire Romance
His Enchanting Princess
His Lovely Prisoner
My Best Friend Forever
A Werewolf Jock for Thanksgiving
Enchanted by You: A Romance Collection
To Have Her: An Alpha Male Romance Collection
You're Mine, Wife
Her Beautiful Captor: A Captive Romance Collection
His Exquisite Prisoner
My First Theft Went a Little Like This
A Werewolf Jock for the New Year
Taking Back My Bride
So Much More
My Immortal Valentine
Short and Not So Sweet: A Short Story Collection
Caught by Mr. Smith
Bad Habits: A MMF Romance
Claiming Lady Wynn
Compromised: A Romance Collection
Over the Moon(cake) for You
The Sweetest Revenge: An Age Gap Romance
Noticed by My Dad's Best Friend: An Age Gap Romance
Bought by My Best Friend's Dad: An Age Gap Romance
Mile High with My Dad's Best Friend: An Age Gap Romance
Dad's Former Best Friend Just Got Out of Prison: An Age Gap
Romance
Bought by My Dad's Boss: An Age Gap Romance
Found by My Bully's Dad: An Age Gap Romance

Wanted by My Best Friend's Dad: An Age Gap Romance
Caught by the King: An Age Gap Romance
Saved by My Professor: An Age Gap Romance
Claimed by a Billionaire on Christmas Eve: An Age Gap Romance
Bought by My Bully's Dad: An Age Gap Romance
Older Than Me: An Age Gap Romance Collection
Wanted by My Ex-Boyfriend's Dad: An Age Gap Romance
Caught by My Dad's Boss: An Age Gap Romance
A Billionaire for Lunar New Year: An Age Gap Romance
To Be His: An Age Gap Romance Collection
Bought by the Billionaire: An Age Gap Romance
Caught by My Boyfriend's Dad: An Age Gap Romance
Discovered by My Best Friend's Dad: An Age Gap Romance
Caught with the King: An Age Gap Romance
Surprised by the Billionaire: An Age Gap Romance
Wedded to the Mobster: An Age Gap Romance
Noticed by My Boyfriend's Coach: An Age Gap Romance
Picked Up by the Mobster: An Age Gap Romance
Kidnapped by the Billionaire: An Age Gap Romance
Caught by My Professor: An Age Gap Romance
Working for My Dad's Best Friend: An Age Gap Romance
Waiting on My Dad's Former Friend: An Age Gap Romance
Trapped in the Storm With My Boyfriend's Dad: An Age Gap Romance
She's Mine: An Age Gap Romance Collection
Claimed by the Mountain Man: An Age Gap Romance
An Offer from My Dad's Creditor: An Age Gap Romance
Knocked Up by the Tycoon: An Age Gap Romance
Caught by the College President: An Age Gap Romance
Wanted by My Fake Boyfriend's Dad: An Age Gap Romance

An Offer from the CEO: An Age Gap Romance

Claimed by the Hotel Owner: An Age Gap Romance

Found by the Cowboy: An Age Gap Romance

Claimed by the Lawyer: An Age Gap Romance

Security Risk: An Age Gap Romance

Prom Night with My Boyfriend's Dad: An Age Gap Romance

Trapping the Billionaire: An Age Gap Romance

My Best Friend's Stepbrother: An Age Gap Romance

My Billionaire Ex-Boyfriend

The Mobster's Property: An Age Gap Romance

Pursued by the Club Owner: An Age Gap Romance

He's Obsessed: An Age Gap Romance Collection

Taken by the Senator: An Age Gap Romance

Alpha Male Alert: An Age Gap Romance Collection

Wanting the Intern: An Age Gap Instalove Romance

Noticed by My Bully's Dad: An Age Gap Romance

About the Author

When I manage to tear myself away from taking Buzzfeed quizzes and watching unhealthy amounts of TV, I write romance and smut. My works feature alpha males, sexy times, and/or my sarcastic sense of humor. I hail from Cleveland, aka the best freaking city in the world, and believe LeBron James is the perfect human being. Despite all of my efforts, I have never truly been able to quit caffeine. My favorites include Taylor Swift, Florence + the Machine, and SHINee. I love to hate/hate to love k-dramas. If I say I'm on a diet, I'm just lying to you and myself. One of these days, I'm going to get hypertension from an excess of salt, both literal and figurative. If I'm awkward around you, I probably don't know what to say to you and/or I think you're hot. And despite what anyone says, Forrest Gump so deserved that Oscar over Pulp Fiction.

www.ingramcontent.com/pod-product-compliance
Lightning Source LLC
Chambersburg PA
CBHW021322160726
47994CB00004B/1570